ALLIGATOR ANCESTORS!

For Ellie the editor, thanks for keeping me in check (well, mostly!)
~ S S

For the dinotastic Sarah M
and Eleanor W
~ A G

GLOOP'S AMAZING POO MUSEUM

Come and see our DINO DOO-DOO!

LITTLE TIGER PRESS LTD,
an imprint of the Little Tiger Group
1 Coda Studios, 189 Munster Road, London SW6 6AW
Imported into the EEA by Penguin Random House Ireland,
Morrison Chambers, 32 Nassau Street, Dublin D02 YH68
www.littletiger.co.uk

First published in Great Britain 2022

Text copyright © Steve Smallman 2022 ∗ Illustrations copyright © Ada Grey 2022
Steve Smallman and Ada Grey have asserted their rights to be identified as the author
and illustrator of this work under the Copyright, Designs and Patents Act, 1988
A CIP catalogue record for this book is available from the British Library
All rights reserved ∗ ISBN 978-1-80104-299-4

Printed in China ∗ LTP/1400/4378/0522

10 9 8 7 6 5 4 3 2 1

FSC
www.fsc.org
MIX
Paper from
responsible sources
FSC® C104723

The Forest Stewardship Council® (FSC®) is an international,
non-governmental organisation dedicated to promoting responsible
management of the world's forests. FSC® operates a system of forest
certification and product labelling that allows consumers to identify
wood and wood-based products from well-managed forests.

For more information about the FSC®, please visit their website at www.fsc.org

This Little Tiger book belongs to:

_____

_____

_____

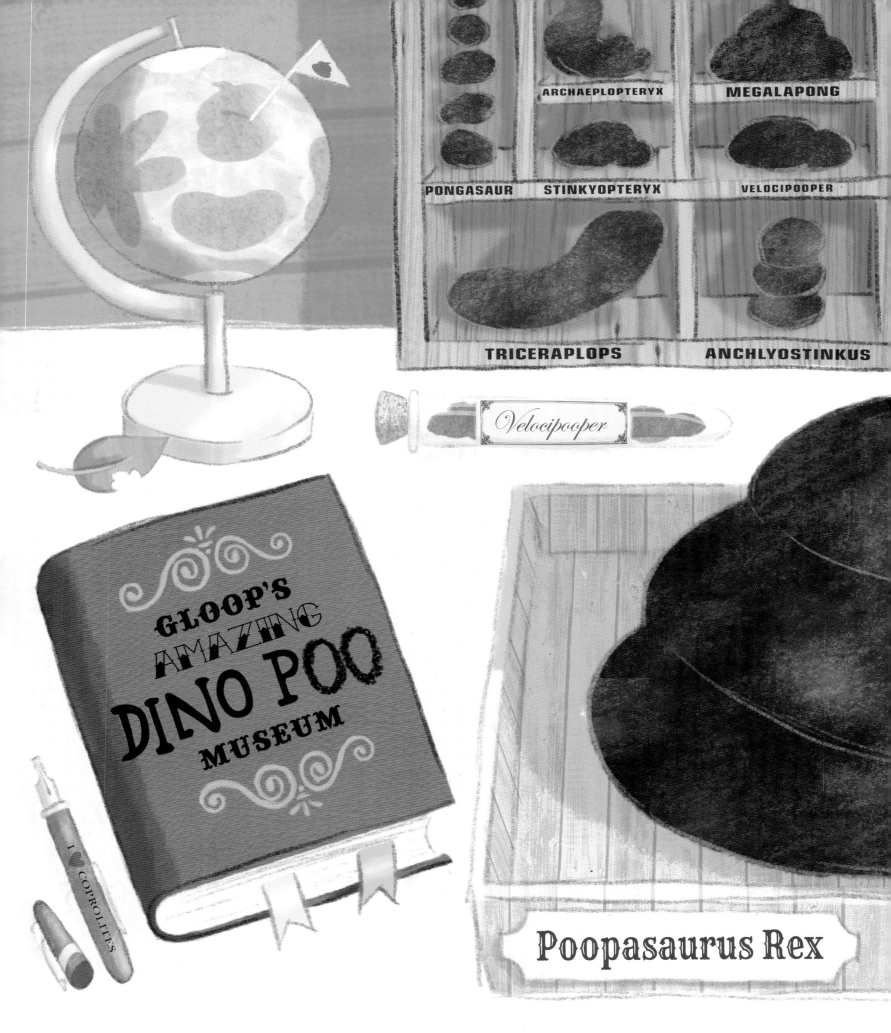

ARCHAEPLOPTERYX

MEGALAPONG

PONGASAUR   STINKYOPTERYX   VELOCIPOOPER

TRICERAPLOPS   ANCHLYOSTINKUS

Velocipooper

GLOOP'S
AMAZING
DINO POO
MUSEUM

I ♥ COPROLITES

Poopasaurus Rex

POO IN THE ZOO

THE ISLAND OF
DINOSAUR POO

MCGrew's
ZOO

Steve Smallman

Ada Grey

LITTLE TIGER

LONDON

Little Bob McGrew and the creatures from his zoo
Were going off on holiday . . . to **where?** Nobody knew!
"Are we going on a train?" they asked. "Or maybe on a plane?"

"Oh no, my friends," Bob chuckled,

"we are travelling by . . ."

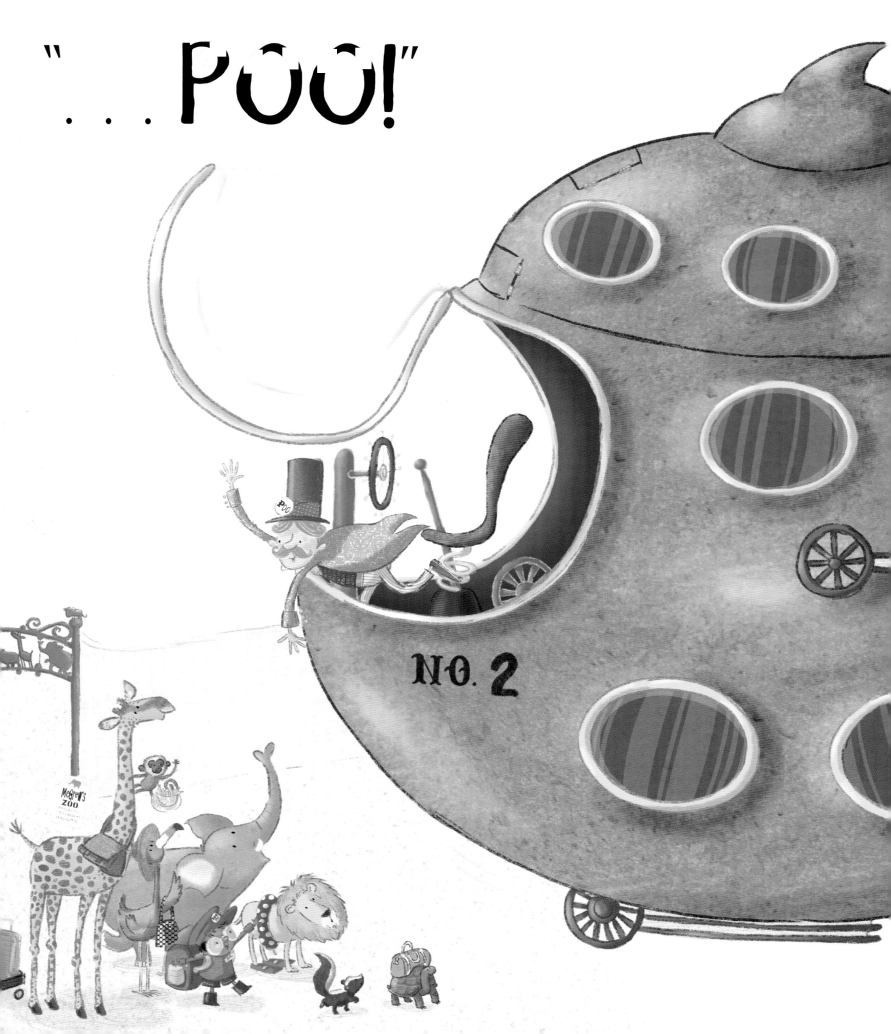

"Hallo there!" It was Hector (Hector Gloop, the **poo** collector).

"We're off on an adventure in my **poo** ship, Number 2!

To the island of Kerplink, where the sea is warm and pink.

A paradise that's also called the Land of Living **Poo!**"

So they quickly climbed aboard and away the floater **soared**,
And Hector Gloop collected **poop** from everywhere they flew.

A stinky pile
of stoat **poo**,

some musty
mountain goat **poo**,

Hare **poo**,

bear **poo**,

and yeti **poo** too!

Dear old Hector never stopped
catching anything that **plopped**,
He **even** had a harness
he could dangle in, too.

Flying through the treetops,
chasing chimpanzee **plops**,

Doo-doo
from a **kinkajou**
and pangolin **poo!**

Then things got very frightening, with **thunderbolts** and lightning,

And wind that rocked the **poo ship** with a tummy-churning motion.

Hector yelled, "Hold tight!" pressed the button on his right,

And steered them quickly down towards the angry-looking ocean!

Then they got a **big** surprise, as before their very eyes,
Their 'ship' became a **submarine** that sank beneath the blue.
And as soon as they went under, everybody **gasped** in wonder,
As all the **startled** underwater creatures did a **poo!**

"Whoopee!" cried Hector Gloop,
as he caught a porpoise **poop**,

And something from an octopus
that really **wasn't** ink!

A tiny little snail **poo**, a **big** pink whale **poo**,

Then through the periscope
Bob spied the island of Kerplink!
They sailed towards the shore
of the island where they saw . . .

. . . Some **dinosaurs** who smiled and said,
"Hello there, who are **you**?"

Bob answered, "Bob McGrew
and the creatures from my zoo,
And Hector Gloop
who's looking for
a pile of living **poo!**"

The dinosaurs all **laughed**, they thought Hector must be daft,
As he listened to each dino **poo** to see if it was breathing.

Then T-Rex cried, "Cooeee!
Would you like to stay for tea?"
"No thanks!" cried Bob, "I'm sorry,
but we really **must** be leaving!"

"Oh no, but I insist!" the Tyrannosaurus hissed. "Tonight, I will be dining on some toast . . . AND ALL OF YOU!"

Then he **chased** them
down the beach,

they were **almost**
in his reach,

When he **tripped** . . . .

. . . and landed head first in the trolley full of **poo!**

On the boat, poor Hector whined,
"I left all those **poos** behind!"
"At least we're safe!" said Bob. "And look!
There's **one** here on the floor!"

Then they got a **big** surprise
as it opened up its eyes . . .
"The Living **Poo?**"
gasped Hector.

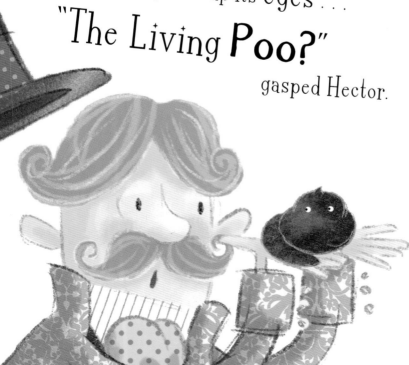

"No, a tiny dinosaur!"

It said, "I've been so lonely because sadly I'm the only

Little dinosaur who's round and looks exactly like a **poop**.

And it seems that, in the end, no one wants a **poo**-shaped friend."

"We'd **love** to be your friends!" said Bob.

"**Me too!**" cried Hector Gloop.

PLOP

WE ♥ U

WELCOME HOME

PLOP

The tearful Ploppasaur gave a joyful little roar,
And decided there and then to go and join them at the zoo.
Now he's **happy** as can be with his big new family . . .

And people flock to catch a glimpse of Plop,
the Living Poo!

More fabulously funny tales from Steve Smallman...

LITTLE TIGER

For information regarding any of the above titles or for our catalogue, please contact us: Little Tiger Press Ltd, 1 Coda Studios, 189 Munster Road, London SW6 6AW ✳ Tel: 020 7385 6333
E-mail: contact@littletiger.co.uk ✳ www.littletiger.co.uk